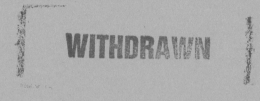

DESERT TOWN

BONNIE and ARTHUR GEISERT

HOUGHTON MIFFLIN COMPANY BOSTON

Walter Lorraine Books

2001

To the people of Montello, Nevada

Walter Lorraine *wr* Books

Text copyright © 2001 by Bonnie Geisert
Illustrations copyright © 2001 by Arthur Geisert
All rights reserved. For information about permission
to reproduce selections from this book, write to
Permissions, Houghton Mifflin Company, 215 Park
Avenue South, New York, 10003.

Library of Congress Cataloging-in-Publication Data
Geisert, Bonnie.
   Desert town / Bonnie and Arthur Geisert.
      p.   cm.
   ISBN 0-395-95387-1
   1. Cities and towns—United States—Juvenile literature.   2. Deserts—United
States—Juvenile literature.   3. Desert people—United States—Juvenile literature.   [1. Cities
and towns.   2. Deserts.   3. Desert people.]   I. Geisert, Arthur.   II. Title.
HT123.G42 2000
307.76'0973—dc21

                                                                00-033605

Printed in the United States of America
WOZ 10 9 8 7 6 5 4 3 2 1

DESERT TOWN

In the vast desert region, the towns are small and far apart. A reliable water source and the need for a supply station between distant points dictated the town sites. Some served early miners and ranchers. Some began as railroad towns where trains no longer stop and where people who love the desert continue to live.

In the middle of miles of brush-covered land outlined by barren hills,
the desert town bakes in the summer heat.

Once a busy rail station for shipping cattle, the town is no longer
a stopping point for trains.

The summer sun is hot and shines on the desert many hours each day.
Everyone stays inside if they can, or they move at a slow pace.

Everything is affected by the sun. Even the dogs move slowly.

Many people work at night when the air is cooler.
Then people can enjoy being outside.

Nighttime is better for active games like basketball, too.

When the sun rises, the family laundry is already hanging on the line.

By the time breakfast is over, the laundry will be dry.
Outside chores are finished before it gets unbearably hot.

Children cool themselves under a sprinkler and dogs find
shady spots to dig holes to escape the heat of the day.

Neighbors linger and visit in the air-conditioned grocery store and gas station.

After a week of hard work, Saturday night is a time to party and dance.

Ranchers and ranch hands come from miles away to join in the evening fun.

Extreme changes in weather are common in the desert.
A fall wind can whip up a sudden sandstorm.

Sand is blown into drifts like snow. Flying sand can peel paint from houses
and can leave pits in glass and windows.

The sand stings the skin. Often, tumbleweeds are tossed into the air and
blown against fences and building corners.

The children play inside to be safe from the roaring wind and stinging sand.
Everyone avoids doing anything outside.

When the weather is calm, stock trucks pass through the town carrying cattle
to market from ranches in the area.

Some stop for gas and food because there are many miles between towns.

When Christmas nears, holiday decorations brighten the town
and business picks up at the gift shop.

Church members don costumes and use animals to dramatize the Christmas story.
Townspeople enjoy seeing live animals and people they know in the Nativity.

Although it's unusual, occasionally the desert town can get heavy snow in the winter.

Then, snow removers rush to clear the roads, although in a very few days
the snow will melt in the warm air.

The patter of a late-winter rain on the roofs and windows
is always a pleasant sound to people.

Even very small amounts of rainwater are important to the quality of life here.

Even the small amount of rain and snow during winter can turn the desert green for a short time in spring. Then, wildflowers bloom with a blaze of color.

The land is renewed. The sound of an airplane motor preparing for flight fills the air.
The children anxiously look forward to summer vacation.

Around the town, people repair and clean their property.

But spring's renewal of the desert has been brief.
Summer is near and already it has become uncomfortably hot and dry.

A year has passed in the desert town. Stories of people at work and play unfold in the illustrations. In the harsh environment, people adapted their work and play. They displayed ingenuity and revealed a spirit of optimism.

One family living near the tracks made several changes during the year. Their home was enlarged to a doublewide bus house. A bigger swimming pool and new slide were added. A new baby boy arrived just before the sandstorm and in plenty of time for the Nativity. A pair of well-worn bib overalls were replaced with new ones.

A taped windowpane shows a downside of playing basketball. The grocery store featured watermelons in season. A pet donkey, who allowed children to ride him and who stood still in the Nativity, has his own small yard.

The deep snow was too heavy for the overhang on the gas station and grocery store, but a lumber delivery means that soon it will be rebuilt. While ruins at the edge of town crumbled, their best years were preserved in photographs. A house and garage were painted, while a house for sale attracted no buyer.

A kiss in the shadows led to a proposal and then a wedding.

After a year of restoration, the airplane was ready to fly, and a new windsock to aid the pilot ballooned in the wind.